BRIGHT and EARLY BOOKS for BEGINNING Beginners

This book belongs to ...

_____

©Illus. Dr. Seuss 1957

Copyright © 1997 by Berenstain Enterprises, Inc.
All rights reserved under International and Pan-American Copyright Conventions.
Published in the United States by Random House, Inc., New York,
and simultaneously in Canada by Random House of Canada Limited, Toronto.

http://www.randomhouse.com/

Library of Congress Cataloging-in-Publication Data
Berenstain, Stan, 1923–
The Berenstains' A book / [Stan & Jan Berenstain].
    p.   cm. — (A bright and early book) |
SUMMARY: An army of angry ants march across and around
all sorts of items that begin with the letter "a."
ISBN 0-679-88705-9 (trade). — ISBN 0-679-98705-3 (lib. bdg.)
[1. Ants—Fiction.   2. Alphabet.]
I. Berenstain, Jan, 1923–   II. Title.   III. Series: Bright and early book.
PZ7.B4483Bfwl   1997   [E]—dc21   97-6783

Printed in the United States of America   10 9 8 7 6 5 4 3 2 1

BRIGHT & EARLY BOOKS is a registered trademark of Random House, Inc.

BERENSTAINS'
A BOOK

Stan & Jan Berenstain

A Bright and Early Book
From BEGINNER BOOKS
A Division of Random House, Inc.

Ant

Ants

Angry ants advance

—across an apple,

across an acorn.

Angry ants
advance across
an apple
and an acorn,

across an apricot,

an ax,

and an angleworm.

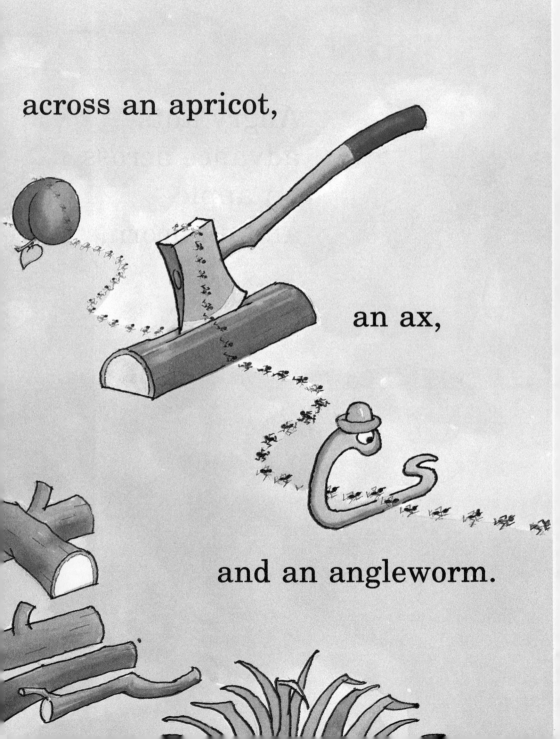

Why do angry ants
advance across
an apple,
an acorn,
an apricot,
an ax,
and an angleworm?

Angry ants
advance across
an alligator

and Aunt Alice's airplane,

and across Avenue A.

Angry ants
advance across
apes' apartments

—and <u>all</u> <u>Arizona</u>!

<u>Why</u> do angry ants
advance across
an apple,
an acorn,
an apricot,
an ax,
an angleworm,
an alligator,
Aunt Alice's airplane,
Avenue A,
apes' apartments,
and <u>all</u> <u>Arizona</u>?

Aha!
An anteater
and
an anthill!

That's <u>why</u>
angry ants advanced
across an apple,
an acorn,
an apricot,
an ax,
an angleworm,
an alligator,
Aunt Alice's airplane,
Avenue A,
apes' apartments,
and <u>all</u> <u>Arizona</u>!

Ants are amazing.

BRIGHT and EARLY BOOKS for BEGINNING Beginners